A LOVE LETTER
FROM A STRAY MOON

Published in UK by Little Toller Books 2014
Lower Dairy, Toller Fratrum, Dorset

First published in Australia by The Text Publishing Company

Words © Jay Griffiths 2011

Cover Artwork © Bridget McCrum 2014

Set in Perpetua by Little Toller Books
Printed by TJ International in Padstow, Cornwall

All papers used by Little Toller Books are natural, recyclable products made from wood grown in sustainable, well-managed forests

A CIP catalogue record for this book is available from the British Library

ISBN 978-1-908213-17-4

A love letter from a Stray Moon

JAY GRIFFITHS

Little Toller Books

DORSET

Foreword

*H*ow to handle this book? The question is not figurative but literal. How to pick it up? Where to place it? How to close it when you have to put it down?

The questions arise because it's so full of love and pain. Its pages are like taken-off bandages. Its spine, like Frida Kahlo's, is damaged. When you turn a page you place a hand on its forehead.

Yet it never winces and in its breathing there is a continuous promise and faith, sometimes tranquil. Sometimes furious.

The image on its cover is of a pair of wings. And maybe one has to handle this book as if it were a bird, a live bird. You walk, and it perches on your shoulder. You shut your eyes, and it takes off into the sky. You sleep and it wakes you before the first light.

It's a small migratory bird who crosses oceans and centuries and carries messages signed by Lorca and Martí and Whitman and you, its reader.

And when it returns it refinds its nest which is the palm between the fingers and thumb of your imagination.

John Berger
Haute Savoie, France

Exiled
from
Casa Azul

I have always wanted wings. To fly where I belong, to become who I am, to speak my truths winged and moon-swayed.

When I was a small girl, I rehearsed my flight. I dreamt of flying. I jumped off walls and flew, but only down. I wanted to fly up; I needed wings. My hope was winged but it wasn't enough. I jumped when I walked and I photographed myself just by blinking, catching the bright flight of the moment, airborne, between each blink. My friends said that I was graceful, that I made little leaps as I walked, so I floated like a bird, but they also teased me terribly, my friends, and cut me out of their games because polio had damaged my leg, and they called me peg-leg. I learned to swear and practised on them as much as I could, telling them they were *hijos de puta* and I was going to the fucking moon.

One evening, the moon rising, I was out playing in the

courtyard and my father called me in, his eyes intense, brimming with the pleasure he knew he was about to give me. My mother hugged me and set me on the floor in front of her.

'My little angel,' she said, and gave me a wrapped box to open. Never patient, I ripped off the packaging and there inside was a white dress with wings like an angel. I gasped with delight—they knew, *they knew*! It was as if they had looked into my heart and seen what I longed for. I tore off my clothes, flung them into the corner and put on the dress, the wings white and perfect at my shoulders. In the soaring moment, with all the transfixed delight which a child can feel, my spirit as fluent as the Rio Papaloapan and my arms unfurled like an eagle's wings, I ran to the courtyard, knowing that I would fly, so I jumped for the moon. And fell to earth, horribly.

I was shattered and broken-hearted, and I sobbed while my parents laughed kindly, 'Oh, Frida, Frida, of course they are not real wings—how could they be real?' How could they *not* be real? I thought, because flight is real and hope is real and magic is real, and I cried furiously. These were more real to me than anything, and I had no wish for substitutes. They ask for flight, kids do, they ask for flight and only get straw wings. I could not fly and it felt as if there were ribbons from my skirts which were nailed into the ground. I could not fly but I had to.

My first memory was of the idea of the moon. Our schoolteacher was weird, with a wig and strange clothes, and she was standing in a darkened classroom while we were hushed with surprise as her face was lit from underneath by a candle she was holding. It jagged her features and jangled her face to a skull, like children on the Mexican Day of the Dead turning themselves into spookies by shining torches up under their chins. In her other hand, she held an orange and she told us that the sun (the candle) lit the earth (the orange) and the moon, but she didn't have three hands and the moon was pure idea, an exile present only in its name. (Present in my mind, though, full and shining.) This was the widening universe, so overwhelming that I pissed myself. The teachers made me take off my wet dress and put on some clothes from another girl and I hated that kid from then on. That night I stared unblinking at the moon until my eyes were watering and I knew I would fly there one day.

Before I flew to the moon, though, I dragged that girl across the road and started strangling her and to this day I remember her tongue writhing out of her mouth. The baker came by and yanked me away from her, but I didn't care because I knew I would fly to the moon and she wouldn't.

I recovered from polio, and I grew fierce, boxing, playing football and swimming, and I remember those days of skates, bicycles and boats as if it was a girl's boyhood, those days when I was as sleek and disobedient as an otter, tempestuously playful and revelling in it. I was sent to catechism class with my sister and we escaped and went to an orchard to eat quinces. I will never forget how sweet was the fruit of our disobedience in that orchard.

I scampered quicksilver through my childhood, out to being a naughty teenager when everything tasted of wine, melons and chilli. I wore a peaked cap and men's suits so they tutted, the neighbours, *who does she think she is?* I scorned them—I scorned all those who scorned me—and I took a cigarette lighter and darted towards the hems of their shawls till they squawked and flapped my hands away. (And the *trompetilla* sniggered to the cactus.) In my gang at college we played havoc, in all the keys of chaos. Cleverer, quicker, droller and better read than most of the teachers, we exploded with anarchy and mischief. We got hold of a donkey, one day, and rode it through the college, falling about laughing at the stale-faces who tried to tell us off. We caught a stray dog and tied it up with fireworks, and lit them so the dog shot off dementedly around the corridors. Poor dog, I thought later. At the time, I was drunk, giggling like a skellington in wellingtons, flowers sprouting from my skull. What flower? *Ix-canan*, in its Mayan name, the guardian of the forest, which they also call the firecracker bush.

I was fifteen and I carried a world in my satchel: books, quotes, notebooks, butterflies, drawings and flowers. I cut my hair like a boy, wore overalls, and my eyes shone with devilry and love. The stale-faces called me irreverent. Absolutely not, I snapped, I revere Walt Whitman, Gide, Cocteau and Eliot, Marx, Hegel and Engels, Pushkin, Gogol and Tolstoy. We were terrible show-offs: 'Alejandro, lend me your Spengler, I don't have anything to read on the bus!' I cried to my clandestine lover. We went busking, playing the violin in the Loreto Garden, listening to the organ-grinders and skating at dawn. In imagination, we climbed the Himalayas, rowed down the Amazon and sauntered across Russia. I read the imaginary biography of the painter Paolo Uccello and adored it so much that I learned it off by heart.

We curled up in libraries eating sherbet, we flirted and argued and set fire to everything which offended our souls. That was how Diego Rivera first heard of me. 'Arm yourself to deal with these kids,' he was told by the other painters. He laughed, incredulous, as they told him what had happened to them. The other muralists had come and painted garbage on our walls; they built a scaffold to overreach themselves and underneath them were wood shavings, paper, bits of oily rags, so we'd set them on fire, obviously. The paintings would be ruined, the painters so pissed off that they took to wearing pistols.

I never needed to trace my roots; I could feel them, inside me, my fallopian tubes were grinning like tendrils of vines, my veins as tough as lianas while my legs grew from the earth, twining up into my body, and my fingers were leaves asking questions of the world of spring, those fingers which would one day find his. My heart turned, heliotrope to the sun, wherever sun was. *El ojo verde*, the green eye, all the Amazon was winking within my eyes, and my mouth was full of *Das Kapital* and poetry. Oh, and the faun, I forgot to say, was my friend. I suckled from the breast of Mexico, before gringos, before Columbus, the milk of the Olmec and the Aztec; my blood is the sap of Mexican plants and my mind is metamorphosing from caterpillar to butterfly, symbol of the psyche.

I was drunk on life, drunk on night which was wicked

with scent, night which lay across my body like Othello's heavy love over Desdemona's sleeping, breathing, dying body. I sucked all the scent from the orange blossom, and the *datura* gave itself to me. I could smell everything; I could smell thoughts and words and colours, vanilla days, vermilion nights. Believe me, I could smell the very sky— *with my teeth.*

I grew up in rays of love from the sun, my father. I lived in the sky (why not?), for my father's house was Casa Azul, the blue house, the house of sky. In those days there was enough sky for everything to fly, and I was always the first to jump. My father's town was called the 'father of springtime' and, as he was the father of my springtime, I was sprung. Those were the days when everything could fly. The curled leaf in spring is sprung in its flight to sunlight, and kittens, cantering up gardens, dew drops from long grass all over their noses and paws, felt their kitten-hearts bursting with sun and life because they knew they could fly. To me, all words were winged and all flight was minded and, since I lived in overflow, I overflew. In those days, I understood Icarus, daring, defiant darling, and maybe like him I flew too high, but the Inca doves cooed me, the crested caracara called and I was caught in a cascade of parrots, a whirring of hummingbirds, whose hearts could beat, like mine, over a thousand times per minute.

And, in one hummingbird heartbeat, it was all over.

I was eighteen. Just a day; the sun rose, the earth turned, but something terrible happened. Did the earth turn too fast, or did I?

Alejandro and I were on a bus. 'Dammit,' I said, 'I forgot my parasol. I must've left it somewhere, let's get off.' We did, and leapt on another bus; that was the reason I was on the bus which destroyed me. I was searching for a parasol, something to shade me from the sun. What on earth was I doing? If only I knew the truths of my own metaphors; I am the moon, and the entire earth is my parasol, protecting me from the sun's rays.

A tiny ex-voto painting, a good-luck charm of the Virgin, swayed by the driver's head till Our Mother was dizzy. It was raining a little outside, and the bus was packed but Alejandro and I managed to find seats at the back. I sat with my hand running dangerously close to his balls, and he was wincing between acute pleasure and acute embarrassment, as several old ladies turned to stare, not quite believing that I was tickling his chestnuts on the bus, and I was starting to giggle at the outraged expressions of the *señoras*.

We were approaching a marketplace which was teeming, even in the rain, and there was a painter on the bus, carrying a packet of gold powder, while a tired child was nudging his nose into the sleeve of one of the cross old ladies, and not one of us knew that this was the moment of scissors, which would cut our lives in two. The route of our bus crossed the tramlines, and a tram—a trolley car—was bearing down on us, as if neither could brake, as if it were all in slow motion, as if it were as inevitable, ineluctable as *El Destino*. *El Destino* held the scissors, one scissor blade the tramlines, one scissor blade the route of the bus.

The bus withstood the impact for a long engulfed moment and then cracked apart, shattering into a thousand pieces, and the handrail broke and speared through my body, piercing my pelvis, and my clothes were torn off me and the painter's gold spilled all over me so I lay like a still life, or an icon, half-dead, half-alive. White skin, red blood and covered with gold, I half-heard someone sob 'look at the dancer,' thinking that I must have just come from a performance, and that the gold was part of my role. A dancer. Never to be that. My Golden Age was over.

The accident was like a hammer breaking my spine, a

chisel carving my life to the bone. The steel handrail which entered my stomach came out through my vagina and my screams were louder than the siren of the ambulance.

All of my afterlife referred always to that *now*, that moment then. Then, when with a shriek, twisted metal and hips, a torture of pulleys and a pool of blood, I was flung away from all I knew and all I had been. The ferocious wrench, the shattering of me. I was flung into the darkness of outer space, injured, lonely, and part of me died—I became the strange and limping moon you see every night. Before, I had been part of earth, as young as life itself and I had known dance and freedom. After, I was unearthed, old as death, and caged in days.

I was taken to hospital, and for long weeks the doctors did not know if I would live. My mind became stale with pain and I could smell no word, no sky, only the horrible hospital opposites of disinfectant and putrefaction. All the green *riqueza* of language in the body was cut down to the dull semaphore of pain while the vultures pecked my liver. If I could never be a dancer, death took on the role, death the dancer curtseying to me all my life as I lived dying. If I was going to fly, from now on it would have to be metaphoric.

Some time after the accident, as I was still in bed, sick

and feverish, with paintbrushes in my hand, I suddenly saw in their delicate, feathered tips the tangent of my flight. My soul could fly with each brushstroke and my paintings could make visible all the universes which my soul held within it.

This was the beginning of my age of loneliness, my Age of Silver. Alejandro left me and my exile was extraordinary, my warm soul caged in a cold bedstead across a deserted sky. I paint in blood and silver, in love and exile. For love is my nature and I am red at heart, but my exile is silver. That is my contradiction and the source of my sorrow, the anguish of the Age of Silver, fallen from the Age of Gold.

I was the first exile of the solar system—a slip of earth, hurled into the sky, flung out alone, too young, too far, too dark. I have recurring nightmares of being cast into space once more, entirely alone, my ears ringing with the white noise of galaxies far beyond any hearing. A strange birth it was. The birth of exile, the death of home. The death of mothering and the birth of a stricken art.

The moon's
Instructions
for Loss

I was born by revolution. According to the register of births, I was born in 1907 but, according to the register of significance, I was the daughter of the Mexican revolution, born in 1910 at the end of dictatorship and the beginning of the peasant revolutions of Zapata.

In the earliest aeons, before she became solid, the earth was a ball of strange gases, and I imagine her like this: if you whistled to the Northern Lights they would swim together, circling in space like a shoal of colours, heat-wraiths stretching, suggesting, dancing backwards, some losing their contact and disappearing, a phantasmic flicker of possibility evaporating into blackness.

And the moon? In the revolution of the earth's turning—and I am a revolutionary—a shard of earth was flung off, coalescing, reforming further and later, far off as the moon. But shard is the wrong word, too hard and substantial; so immaterial was this moment, so unearthly the earth, so unanchored the moon, what word would be better? The moon was more like Idea, more like Metaphor, or Time, Flight or Potential or Longing. A highly strung intensity of latency.

The moon, shining on the Lacandon jungle and Mexico City, on Havana and Madrid, Buenos Aires, Santiago, Montevideo and New York, is wearing a ski-mask and is rolling a cigarette with tobacco she nicked from the *subcomandante* while she writes a communiqué to earth. 'Instructions for Loss,' it begins. There are many kinds of revolutions and many of these are invisible: when loss has razed the psyche and despair seems to have massacred the spirit, insurgents of hope sometimes arm themselves in the jungles of the heart.

Picasso famously said: 'I do not seek, I find.' What about those whose distinctions are not between seeking and finding but between losing and being lost? Not caught between Picasso's optimism of seeking and success of finding, but stuck terribly between unfinding and breakage?

Instructions for loss: if you lose something you can find it fractally—and indeed you must find it like this. In order to avoid bitterness, you must find what you lost a thousand times over, in other faces in the moon, other disguises, under other ski-masks, other mountains, not in fractured crystal but in the perfect refraction of a rainbow and the reflection of mirrors, seeing you in myself, myself in you. It is, as it were, a Zapatismo of the human heart, an intuition of plurality which is a salvation, an aesthetic and a rebellion.

To Diego
and All Who
have Wings

I glimpsed Diego first when I was just a kid, long before the accident. He was painting *The Creation*, and I saw him as a man unbowed by any god for he knew he was man the creator. I saw coasts in him, volcanoes and forests, a geography of mind painted in all time, from the long pre-Columbian *verde* of forest-mind in its thousands of generations before the peculiar regency of history. And that is the time in which I write now, to plead in those longest cycles of time, for now as I write this, my love letter from the moon to man, I am using my heart as a palette and painting in my own blood.

This is a love letter to Diego, and this is not a love letter to Diego. It is universal and wholly personal. It is dated Right Now, and yet it is as old as the primordial. You, Diego, it is to you. 'Diego is the name of love,' I wrote. But I ask you to read it with many names, whatever your name is that you live by, and let me address myself to your soul, in the simplicity of love, in the generosity of life. To you, then, by all the names of man you ever took, before and before and before, pre-Columbian, pre-literacy, and yet readers too in the strange and unpredictable future, in tenses I am frightened to use. I know you by the flame in your heart, by the light in your eyes, and I write to tell you what I can see, so far from you in fact, so near to you in love. Diego is the name I use to knock on the door of your heart. Yet the door is not the door to his heart alone, but the door to any hearing heart. I take my guitar, and pick out the sound of his name by playing the strings which spell him. But I could play that tune in the key of any name.

And I am Frida but also I am not Frida. I am her paintings and the nature of her love. I am her shadow. I am many women, I answer to many names, any who knows grief. I am all the phases of the moon, I am all her qualities. I am *El Duende*, I am the light of the psyche, writing from my soul, speaking to the psyche of humanity, the psyche which is shaped like the wings of a butterfly or a moth; fly closer, fly nearer to me. After the accident, I was caged in plaster casts for months and on this hard shell I drew butterflies as my first votive painting, encouraging the soul to crack the carapace one day and fly free to the moon.

Years afterwards I met him again, so long ago that it was only yesterday or tomorrow even. I went to ask his advice about my paintings. He marked me and told me later that I looked brilliant as an eagle, my eyes were talons to catch the world I painted. Stock-still, he gazed at me as if there were an entirely new light in his mind's sky. My mind staggered a moment at the acuteness of the sight, the sudden prospect I had not known, seeing his eyes so undefended, so open, sweet as a child and ungated as the Amazon. The door is never locked so I walked straight in.

On the instant, I knew that his soul was of ferocious consequence to mine: I knew that his meaning endlessly mattered to my mind. Something leapt in my womb, like a turning tiny baby. So young his huge eyes, shining and laughing; babyface, moonface, my father, my child—he was all generations to me, all but one.

When I first saw him, I loved him, Prometheus, Maui the Trickster who steals fire, flame-stealer, fire-smuggler, I remember no spark, only fire from the start. He was feral and full of furious love, his words had teeth, his curiosity was a monkey wrench, tearing up half-truths, forcing open unknowns. He defied the standard, dared to detonate the paved path and find the green roaring beneath, he exploded his own mind (because it was there). He refused obedience. No one could ever tell him what to do, so he authored every word of his life, carving the ceaseless demand of the self's absolute authenticity onto the stone of every single day.

'Every time he turns a corner, he is moon-struck, and you would be the moon,' my friend said to me. He dared to stare at the moon and I silvered his eyes, but I also gazed back, unable to look away, mesmerised by him. If he was moon-struck by me, I was lightning-struck by him, with his lightning cast in passion, electric in his hand, a stave thrown in love across the moon-mad miles, so he cracked my breastbone, broke open my heart, made it bigger for love of him.

I fell for him. '*Mamá*, look, the moon's fallen out of the sky.' And there it lies, surprised, swollen on the edge of the world, the lip of the moon kissing the horizon's smile. A man I could cradle, plump as the Buddha, in my arms. Diego, your name means 'supplanter, he that replaces'; he supplanted my loneliness and replaced my exile with love.

I was captivated. I walked across the sky, we talked for ten hours and then I put my hand on his arm and finally said what I came to say: I demand to know you. A demand of my daemon, to find my own shamans, to love the oceans and to know him. A polite but non-negotiable demand.

I should never have come but I had absolutely no choice. It was dangerous enough to meet him once and it was a hundred times more dangerous to walk the road to his door to begin a magnum opus of the soul. I was his lodestar as he was mine, we pulled each other with an ineluctable magnetism and, although it was an almost unbearable love, it was inevitable, for how could his singularity not have cried out to know how my strange and single light shines? How could I, parched, thirsting for life so near me yet so far, not have wanted to drink his liquid mind? I held his face gently in my two cool hands, tilted it towards my lips and drank and drank, but this was not a thirst I could slake and I was as insatiable for him as the moon is for water.

The song of my desire was louder than I could contain, like a wren, seemingly too small for the hugeness of its elation. My mind flew to him habitually, flitting always to the same branch of the same hedge. The blackbird must sing the dusk and the clouds must fill and swell till they ache and rain, and the tree root must crack whatever clay is in its way. So must I, so must. The smell of him. Must must have its way, in urgent, argent, silver desire.

Every month I dazzled him, making him sleepless with desire. I aroused him and crazed him and unminded him. I didn't suggest: I demanded, and this demand was dementing. He ransacked the moon, every muscle of mine he wrung for its pleasure, and afterwards was left only sweet lassitude and a smiling sleep, and my glistening cunt was moonlight shining its own silver in the same night. (My body paints, every month, a still life. Just one red streak of blood across a white page. *Still death*. It is part of my bleak fiesta, my mordant carnival.)

We kissed under the streetlights and our passion was electric: each lamp we kissed under suddenly went off, and only when our lips parted did it switch back on again.

This was the Age of Cobalt: electricity, purity and love. I bent his bowstring taut, compelling his passion, in the tangent of aspiration, the tension of slant in the stretch of mind. In the furthest reach of the body, my orgasm in his arms made me arch my back like a jaguar; his psyche drew together with mine and we yawned like lions.

His reckless intelligence delighted me, his naughty clowning in the aisles for centuries till I split my sides laughing—he tickled my fancy, triggering a ripple effect across the whole of the Pacific, a million tiny waves rilling round a trillion tiny inlets. He was the starriest thing I could see in any direction. We were Popocatépetl and Iztaccíhuatl but, in spite of our love, we were also catastrophic for each other; the second-greatest accident of my life was him.

He would walk even when he didn't know where his walking would take him, compelled to blaze his singular trail, taking a machete and carving his way through to tomorrow morning. His was a hunting mind, nomadic, curious, exquisite to me, sought after, sought out and, while my nomadism was forced on me, he chose his for himself, his superb, undestinationed journey, his utter faithfulness never to stop. And in this we co-fascinated. He, trapeze artist, soloist: I on the single swing of my trajectory. My arc of light in the sky, his pioneer path on earth. Yet he was so paradoxical—part nomad, part tree, becoming rooted in the earth, his deep and dear home, and anchored in myth, buying pre-Columbian idols of stone and clay, greedy for them as he was greedy for women. Not just me.

He was born with the wings of laughter and the gift of flame, fire-stealer for sure and hell-raiser by repute. I alone knew him as a hearth-maker. Wherever he went, he carried a hearth in his hands and a path in his mind, the hearth the always, the path the onwards, so he stayed forever in one place and was forever on the move. I loved him for his inflammability, because I saw his fire everywhere, even in the frozen north, igloos cosy within, glowing pale yellow from a lamp of moss and seal fat.

He played all parts, gardener and gypsy, carpenter and cook, artist of the ordinary, the nation's most famous painter, shaman and fool, physician and metaphysician, drummer of the night and dreamer of the day, a dangerous, beautiful creation, dissolute scamp, chief mischief-maker, wanderer, artist, tramp. His nomadic longing mind wanted more: more path, more sky, more moon, more myth, more women. He looked up.

I was mute except through mouths other than my own and my only voice was my light, my speechless eloquent silverlight, so words like wings alighted meaning on silent white paper. The moon was the first author, the writer who never spoke aloud, and man was full of language and my silence piqued him. What was my meaning and how did I voice my shine? How did I author the tides and spell my passion? With what gravity and what levity did I write my courses? How did I howl the wolf, and why the howl? (I can tell you: the wolf, then a sweet cub batting the violets with its too-big paws, is now an old wolf howling over the bones.)

His languages delighted me: bravura, plethora and plenty; Babel, cornucopia and harvest; barnfuls of abundance, basketfuls of onions and armfuls of icons. His mind was mint-green in every new trefoil of leaf, another mile, another language, and his words romped all over the world, rafting across Polynesia, drifting sacred in Sufi whispers, taking wing from the Amazon and rambling thoughtful across the grasslands of Argentina. I watched him for thousands of years, willing him on, disobedient, conscious, rude. Ignore the dumb god, get a stonking hard-on, smash the icons and die, if you must, with your panache intact.

I loved him entirely because that is my nature, whole and perfectly circled, and he asked me to marry him— so, on a sudden hillside, a sudden outlaw vow which was an eternal marriage and a lifelong separation too. I am seared by separation, as if there are square brackets round my heart, putting my love in parenthesis, punctuated by his other loves. They said ours would be a difficult love, perhaps an impossible one, because the man is not supposed to fall in love with the moon. The moon didn't mean to and nor did the man. It would have been tidier if they had never met, and more convenient, but the fire so flat, the path so unsung, the woods so unenchanted, the night so undrummed.

If Diego was in his studio, I took him lunch every day in

a basket covered with flowers and I braided flowers into my hair, with rings on all my fingers, and I wore Tehuana skirts, embroidered and ribboned, dressing to make my presence defy my exile, to make my beauty defy my pain. At home, every day I made the table into a still life, piling painted bowls full of fruit which the chipmunk tried to snatch, filling clay pots with flowers which the parrot pecked at, displaying the tortillas on decorative plates which the dogs licked while the osprey watched from her perch on my shoulder. Even when I had no appetite, I feasted on the sight.

I wanted ribbons to tie myself to life. Look at all the ways we are tapestried into life, the delicate intricacy of the threads, vines, tendrils, ropes, tresses, cords, tubes, veins, strings and fingers. Words, too, are tendrils, reaching from my mind to his. I had a thought; a vine of thought curled around my psyche and I wrote to him—an offshoot of the vine—the words transposed into the thread of ink which twists up to his mind, making him smile, his smile a broad line across his face, and he telephones me, the telephone wires such sensitive threads that I can hear him smiling; come over, I said, he came, his quizzical fingers asking questions of mine, yes, my fingers answer, leading his down to the dark jungle vines of my sex, which telegram their delighted replies up to my brain. And after, eyes closed, the air has invisible skeins which link his heart to mine, while beyond me, beyond him, it is the same thread, *La Vida*, life itself which ties us to every plant, every animal. Under the different surfaces, the same thread of vitality, hence the Aztec prayer: 'I am the feather, I am the drum and the mirror of the gods. I am the song. I rain flowers, I rain songs.' And the rest is just painted bread. I am this metamorphosis: I am a deer, I am a mountain, my fingers are vines, and flowers bloom in my hair.

Once, we arranged to meet at the movies, but the crowd was large and I couldn't find him anywhere. Then I heard someone whistling the first bar of the '*Internationale*' and immediately I whistled the second bar and stopped, my face gleeful; he whistled the third, I the fourth and so on until we found each other. The '*Internationale*'. The entire world. If I say he became the entire world to me, what does that mean? That everything I touch is him, everything I see is him. The colour of sky is him, the sound of the accordion and the blue guitar, the spikes of cactus, and the smell of cloves in the pillowcases is him.

He drew his hands around me, cat's-cradling me without touching me, in strands of invisible silk, casting spells of protection and painting the air with strange patterns of healing, holding me as if I were an Aeolian harp and, without touching the strings, with his breath he sang my strings to song. I heard Orpheus those nights when we fucked, knuckled together like a chestnut while our eyes were bright like nutshine in the bedding leaves of the woods.

If there were too many clouds, he tore them down, Prospero to the task, a simple trick of the light, a conjury of the sun, because he was a wonder-worker, thaumaturge. I have watched him make matter out of dream, like the day when he pasted a rainbow on the sky because it was looking a bit bleak. He transformed realities, going under them to the poetics beneath, and under the poetics the physics, and under the physics the transmuting energies, that sound, for instance, can alter matter (and how he was a whistler of worlds), and always, though, under the transmuting energies, was the sweetest alchemy of love for all things. From soil he learned the truths of love and in the earth of his own heart he knew what slender epistles the seedlings write, appealing to the sun, and what need the human soul may have at different seasons, the greenhouse now, the prairie then, the dagger mountain from time to time.

So conjure me starlight, Prospero, and I will wear it like

a jacket. Take a cloud, sewn with blossom, and I will sleep under it like a mohair blanket. Weave me a spellbound home and I will nest in it like a bird in its own spring. Throw me madness like dice, you clown, and I will wear my knickers on my head like a tea cosy isn't and use a biscuit for every other simile. Come to me cockhard and stun me with desire and I will outglow the embers for days. Kiss my lips as we part as they do parting joy from sorrow (*alegría, miserere*), and I will take the descant part on an old school recorder and play my way to heaven.

My passion electrifies the domestic and that is why, when he leaves, the candles gutter, the fire goes grey, the cats keen for him, and the flowers huddle chilly in the vase, when he leaves, when he leaves. How many times did he leave me before he left me?

To take his hand I would have to measure every inch in miles, but to take his mind there is no distance—all these moon miles between us are thinner than a leaf skeleton. He touches me more than I can say, floating his poems in the waters of my soul, lying circled wet and lovely in his dreams and, as I sway the tides without touching them, so I became influent in him. I cannot touch him now but I trickled into his veins and melted into his mind so I became his delicate intricate, his inner intimate, his co-inspirator. Am I still? I don't know. But I know that he is both the silk of my tears and the reason for them.

We, gleaners of time, pick up the unharvested moments. *NOW!* And he seized a scrap of pure serendipity—a charred piece of newspaper in the courtyard which contains only that one word *now!* On the now of midsummer's day, we lay in a hazy fusion of all our Junes, the day the guests didn't show up but, oh, Walt Whitman did. I lay next to him, my womb so moist, so warm, so kindly dark that I thought any gardener would want to plant bulbs in it. Diego did not, and his reluctance bewildered me.

Sometimes we drank our way to insatiable childhood. Glee in me and pond-jumping, boisterous with love for him, I careered around noisily as a seven-year-old on a tricycle playing a tin drum. He made me snort with laughter when he picked up six pebbles, saying they were in search of some earwax. Suntanned and lying on my back on the grass, knees muddy and socks crumpled, me giggleful and naughty. I am a boy. All boys are brothers, and how I love my brothers. I am seven, seventeen and forty-seven, and he loves all my ages as I love all his.

Garrulous, hungry for food and women, tubby, he slept in the bathtub and I loved to bathe him, to put toys in the water, to use sponges and flannels and rosewater and orange, and him so smallboyish until his fountain-flower decided to play too. Another time, sharing a bath, we sat sideways, watching miniature rally cars, cakes and small animals rocket past on the racetrack of the bathmat and he, aged five and a half, lay under a stripy towel in a DIY sauna, while he, aged forty-five and a half or sixty-five and a half, cried serious tears which broke through his face, rock them in though he did. 'Why can't we really live? Do we lack the courage for it? I want to *really live.*' So do I, my love, and I watch over him as if he were the child I had not had.

He despised the merely managing, subsistence farming of the soul because he demanded to live by the electric passion, to let his body turn tidal, not walking pick-peck-pick on the mealy-mouthed pavement. I too demanded to really live, and we lived out our feral passion like teenagers; going to the market one day he threw me backwards and laughing across the stalls and nearly fucked me in full view of all the gawping shoppers. You want to love me? Do so. Quick now. Slip your strong keen up under my long red, feel my warm wet. And then come my gasp. But I wanted to live all my ages, not only as a teenager but as a mother and a grandmother. My friends said he was selfish and cruel, being so unwilling to have a child with me, but fatherhood was not his forte. He fathered his art. And my child was him.

But do not think I serenely accept this. Do not ever call me tranquil. You can keep your moonlight sonatas—I don't recognise myself in them. I can't take this kind of solitude any more.

To be wholly immaterial is too lonely. Must I stay forever so fucking ethereal? Why can't I matter, materially? Why can't I be beflowered? Why can't I spend a few years making cakes and splashing? Why can't I be a fucking lovely ordinary lovely fucking woman? I want to slope off to a bar, warm my hands by the stove, I want to be sleepy with wine, my head on his soft shoulder, as round as a baby's, and I have a sweet, swollen, musky kind of longing to kindle my own kitten. Any scraggy farm cat is allowed her litter of kittens, but not me; I am a stray moon at the back door, mewing for a crescent kitten. The door is slammed against me. 'It's only the moon. Should be fucking neutered.'

All women wanted to mother him. (And fuck him.) Peter Pan, I called him, because I knew him as both child and age-old Pan, goat-god, satyr, erotic to the hilt, genius of the groves, god of the groins, wickedness in the wink. Lascivious as Jean Genet but still as lucent and innocent as the sleeping Endymion, the man given eternal youth because the moon was his lover and came down nightly to embrace him as he slept on the mountain. And the moon bore him daughters.

We only saw each other truly, nakedly, at night, in the darknesses of space and in the little unlinked hours, uncounted, unaccounted by anyone but us, the dark jewels. An elfin love, a faerie love, magically true, actually unreal, but rawly corporeal as the memory of his cock in me sent flutters through the muscles of my cunt for days afterwards.

The first of these jewels was a midnight hour. He had asked about my mind and I had answered about my cunt. How not, if I was to answer him truthfully? You speak in blood and silver, he said. If we drink from the same red cut-glass cup, his lips touching the red glass and the red blood, then we ('Drink to me only with thine eyes') share a passion and a feral mystery. ('Or leave a kiss but in the cup, And I'll not look for wine.') Let's face it, most people don't do things like that. I was mad, and I had the true lunatic's lunar alibi. How the full moon shone that night.

I was born in tidalism, as the earth was changing from liquid to solid, one huge tide of swirling swept off the earth and coalesced as moon. Being tidal myself, I willed his tides to their fullness and I surged over his flood defences, breaching his sea walls so he could not keep me out. I was his madness and his magic and his muse, I was his devotion and his devastation and his devouring passion. I could walk through walls, swim through them, so no air or water or brick could stop me, and when his soul was lost I could find it, curl up next to it and sleep in its arms.

I was an inverse thief in the night: I stole nothing from anyone but I stole into everything, I gave myself away, shedding myself till I waned to nothing, a blank edge of darkness. I stole in through his eyes to his thoughts and I crept in through windows, or through the sky, stealing into his body, an extra ever-undiscovered mineral in the nature of my light, so my quicksilver slipped into his head, and the mad hatter was moon-maddened. Draw down the moon till the tropics are glades of liquid silver and know that the moon has a wingspan the size of the world while the wingtips of madness brush the wind whose own madness in turn stretches the wings tauter. So a gale-force wind and an angle of feather reach further for another wing-inch of turbulence till, at the point of maximum tension, the hurtling bird is almost torn apart by the force of the storm. Almost.

I was as naked as the moon to him. I was, in fact, inside

out. Raw, willingly so, shivering with exposure, my cunt was open to his gaze and my heart open. In one nightmare, I shouted to him for help and all that real day my real throat was hoarse from the shout, my real mind reeling with need for him, for even the moon can be frightened by stalking starshadows which flicker in her nightmares.

I have gazed at his face for thousands of years, his windward, fireward, forward, pathward face, a mountain face I have explored and watched, and behind the snowy boulders I have seen the deepest and softest and rarest thing—the blue eyes of a snow leopard gazing back.

For him, all the world became eager. The pip would willingly sprout, the fish would dance which had only swum before, the rain would jump which had only fallen before. Tender to all aspiration, he lent the saplings a hand. His mindlight flooded the world like a director with whom every actor is in love and women couldn't help but respond, which I understand because the *world* couldn't help but respond: the tiniest spider ran arpeggios for him, the Nile burst its banks, the Amazon forest went on the razzle for him, the bee sucked harder for nectar when he cherished its diligence. Midnight never knew herself till him, but then she dressed in deep-blue velvet and shared a tequila or three, all for his sweet charisma, his

49

charm, for he was the quickener of what was inheld. He saw meaning in all things and so made the world matter in mindedness. Before him, any old dawn would do. He appeared and sunrise increased the voltage because of the unique warmth of his gaze and the dawn chorus turned up the volume because of the quality of his listening. The rainbow began life with just two colours, red and violet, but seeing the wash of pleasure in his eyes it flung in five more, and then the countless shades between. The mountain robin never knew quite who it sang for till he watched as it fluffed up its breast feathers for the best-ever robin boast and he, of course, spoke fluent robin, so he understood it perfectly, and as his face was creased with kindness, lined with story, and crumpled with love, I wanted to make my nest with him, I wanted my belly plump with a swelling egg. I never understood why he was so reluctant.

I was there at his beginning. If I did not exist, the life of mankind would have been only mundane, lovely but ordinary. He could build his hut, collect his water and pick his fruit, a creature of the day only, and happily so but a little lacklustre. I never took away his dayness but I flooded him with an insight of shadows, a feral lustre, that light not of the mind's eye but of the mind's loins.

Wild licence. I can affect the lives of mussels and the pull of tides, but no mind knew I did that until him. Wonder riddles our love. No wonder I loved him: his wondering mind was the first mind on earth to know the iridescence of my wonderlight.

Metaphor began because he loved me—and I am the first metaphor. He was charged with it, swollen with it, metaphor forced its way out of him, a spurt of seed, each glittering and dancing, minute and yet magnificent, the pip invisible and invincible, microcosmic yet containing new worlds a thousand times over, each seed a seed-syllable of speech, lighting the air with a cascade of starlight which fizzes on my tongue. All is metaphor—I am the moon, but I am not the moon. He is Diego, but much more truly he is all of mankind. I am one woman, but I am every woman who understands loss. I am Frida and I am not Frida. We are both fractals, shapes which can be divided into countless self-similar shapes, because all human hearts are fractal like this. True and yet just a metaphor in a world of metaphors. Metaphor is itself a metaphor, a carrying-across, as a child would carry a star in his cupped hands across a room to show his father. 'Look, Papa, look how I made a star and when can we go to the moon?'

He was a child of starlight, child of no one: I was the mother of no one so I elect my children. There are always substitutions, elliptical ways by which the psyche survives and so *he* was the child I carried, cupped in the moon's womb. If I had a child, it was him, sweetest, moon-struck child, let me carry him for months inside me. In our difficult dream, I am the moon, mother of gods, mother of Diego, in all his incarnations, mother of humanity. That's how it is in Mexican mythology, and the sun is the fertiliser, but this was the role he refused, so the sun became my son, my child. I wanted to give birth to him; he was the big pale baby lying in my lap. His fat-man breasts were like the chubby breasts of a baby and I nuzzled my nose into his armpit to smell him like a tigress sniffs her cub.

In moonlight and in metaphorlight, all things are translated, carried across. A star is a seed is a child is a syllable, and he, shapeshifter, is them all, metamorphosing—moving from one form to another. But he was not the first metamorphosis. I was. He was the first to see it. From metaphor he took wing and made myth, magic, mystery and mindedness, art and abstraction and paradox. (I am cold but I make passions burn, I am white but I make red blood flow. I am parched but all the wetness of all the oceans on earth see-saw for me.) A seed, a star, a syllable, a child. They are all the same. All potential. All needing what I can give them, what I am: Time. I am ever unripe, I never flower but I produce ripeness, bloom and burgeoning. I am the original entelechy.

My light was the melody of time and my changes were time's rhythm. His first abstraction was time and he could only have known it through me. I gave him a calendar of changes: a possible future, a realised past, a present of pure potential. I am never the same, so he looks for me every evening and every evening I have turned again, but never turned away from him. Except once.

It was around me and about me that he first whispered his shamanic realities. I drew mystery in the sky for him and he drew me magic on earth, meeting me every month in the language of fire and mind. Because I seemed inexplicable he needed myths to explain me and so for my sake he stepped into the magic of his role. He alone would be self-aware in my light because I gave him the night and he understood the invisible world because of me. Myths glimmered in the dark, will o' the wisps across the marches of the mind flickering *am I real?* Never so. *Am I true?* Always.

And I stretched out my arms and glided into purity utterly translated as he stroked my white body on a bed of white sheets and white sheepskin. He planted the flowers of innocence and those flowers flew, for in those days all flight was innocent, and afterwards, in a lassitude of limbs after flight, he folded me into sleep, tucked the sheets round me, spread his wingspan of swans across me and under the shadow of his wings I slept and dreamt of flying. I have seen his wings, those plump, white wings. I can never forget that, my angel.

He saw how weary I was of exile. He saw how I cried to come home, to come in from the cold night. He saw my oddest, longest, most elliptical loneliness. He saw I had friends and lovers but that I ached for the fireside, for the *lares* and *penates*. He saw I could be all the more free if I had a home, how my hard dance might become more beautiful if I had the grace of a chance to balance on one lovely corner of land, so he folded me into his home.

If a piece of the moon fell into someone's lap, what would they do? Most people would put it back. Not out of unkindness but just not really knowing what to do with it. The moon's quite a handful, a bit of a challenge, a high-maintenance girlfriend, who goes wonky every month, plays havoc without meaning to, she is a force of chaos which messes up order. But he, with a piece of the moon fallen into his lap, gazed at it for a few weeks, then tenderly tucked it into his softest pocket saying: I think it will be better off there. Most men wouldn't make a home with moonlight: too much blood and silver. He gave me love and home, those two things for which I starved. I came home to his *lares* and *penates*, the pre-Columbian statues, and he came home to mine. I found a one-word poem by the fireside. It said 'hearth'. So I wrote it out in orange, all that a hearth contains. Heat. Art. Eat. Hear. Earth. Heart. What more? Hart. My soul longs for you as the hart yearns for the stream, the psalm says. He left me longing, and this is my *Desideratum*. I am half-Catholic, after all, and the mother of sorrows has moved into the attic of my mind.

The years yearned their turnings into love, layer on layer of love laid down in leaves and straw, layers of books re-read, well-loved jokes re-told, boots lovelier with age and use. And for me too he laid layers of love, making tortillas, holding my frightened hand, yelping with glee in the rain, stroking away a headache, cooking me supper, teasing me, enchanting me in glades of twilight, keeping me company in coffee, in toast, in wine, in sadness, in candlelight, in kindness, in carouse, in sobriety, in the most ordinary and therefore the most extraordinary handmade and weatherworn days of home. It was all I wanted, all but.

I lost a child. I had always imagined that my womb was

like a verdant bed of green leaves, glistening, but now I have learned that it's more of a bomb site, the broken glass and concrete of my shattered pelvis stabbing any tiny baby who tried to nestle a moment there. Bleeding and weeping, I painted that loss. I made history, as he said: 'Never before had a woman put such agonised poetry on canvas.'

Everything I love is tied together, and the world is threaded with roots, filaments, fingers, the veins and bloodlines, those ancestral ribbons, tying grandmothers to granddaughters. From life death blossoms, and from death life engraves itself again, but not for me because I am entirely cut from that tapestry now, outside that cycle, further than I can tell you. Those scissors in the hand of *El Destino*, one scissor blade the tramline crossing the blade of the bus, cut the red ribbons of the generations within me. I could have been not only a mother but a grandmother, and an ancestor too, one who would have shone. I could have been part of life's veins and promises. *El Destino* refused.

I watch my sister now, knowing all her little deaths from which more life comes, but mine is a breathing death, an elliptical life, foreshadowed before my time, lit silver when I want to be green. The vine of the ancestors twists up from earth towards me—two little children who adore me as aunt——and I lean as far as I can without falling, but it is hopeless. The green and the red will never know me now.

So, then, I have no child and the terror of that loss I cannot face but I have to see it every day and every night, gazing on my sister earth, mother of all that I would love. I circle her, pale and beyond envy for what I cannot have. She has surpassed me in almost every way, in profusion, in plenty; the primordial sculptor. How she is fecund, how she is happy, while I am empty and barren as Lorca's orange tree. Though I turn the cycles of warm time for all women, I am stuck in a coldness, as if winter had welded itself to the axle of the year and the wheel had stopped turning and spring wouldn't come.

I loved her before humanity existed. I grew up with her, nestling planets held in the gravity of love. Earth, my luckier sister, my happier sister, my sister of rivers, my sister of the green-velvet dress, my sister trilling children quicker than you could sing half an aria from *The Magic Flute*, my sister of sunfuls of warmth, my sister of all fertilities, my wet, wet sister, rich with, oozing with, glistening with. Moisture, life and springingness.

I am not jealous, I have never been envious. I wish her only more blossom, more oranges, more goats, more children, but my grief becomes inconsolable every month. So inconsolable that I drench the earth, for if I must weep with loss I will not bleed alone—I will tip the oceans sideways so they share my kinetic, mad, electric blood. *La Llorona*, the woman weeping by the river, looks to me and, when I cry, the rivers burst their banks. I have no soil for seed, not a drop of water and I know no harvest. Though I bring all things to their fullest potential, in me there is no quickening life, no possibilities. I applaud my sister but I am anguished for more than my narrow slice of sky.

I would have chosen to be Cuaxolotl, goddess of the hearth, but I was made Coyolxauhqui, goddess of the moon. As such, I am always exiled, on the brink of mind and light. Does it matter how I yearn for the hearth or for green day and fullness, round belly and fruitness? He came to love my lips for the language they write across the sky in the mind's light—I have lips, yes, but no smooth pelvis to hold the thunder of birth. It is already cracked. I have the hips of a boy, and I am vividly barren, my eternal, strange unfuckedness.

I painted my barrenness and the fertility of the earth. 'Children are the days, and this is where I end,' I wrote, but it wasn't true, and anyway children adored me: I treated them as equals and they in turn—with greater generosity—treated me as an equal of theirs. I masked my longing with pets: dogs and cats, monkeys, doves and parrots, an eagle and a deer.

Cosmic and telluric, external and internal, I painted my own myth, that I must give birth to myself. If I can't physically be a mother then I must begin my motherhood in the most metaphysical way possible. I painted like no one else and, as a painter, I gave birth to myself. My paintings, he said, were 'acid and tender, hard as steel and delicate and fine as a butterfly's wing, loveable as a beautiful smile, and profound and cruel as the bitterness of life.'

I painted the desert of my days, for I was deserted and lonely, limping through my life. Limping? Did I say limping? Not limping but striding firmly from crisis to crisis. And when my pain made him sad and guilty I'd draw mischievous pornographic sketches which made him snort with laughter, bullfrog honking in the pond.

The left side of my body is painted darkly now, with the moon in tears by my head. Once, I painted myself holding my palette in the form of my heart, painting my vulnerability with my heart's blood. Now it is different. I paint myself, holding my palette as if it were a shield. My art alone is my protection, shielding me from the pain of loss.

If you Are Too Easily,

Dangerously,

Enchantable

I created a bed, a four-poster bed with skeletons on top, surrounded by shells and under the canopy I put a glass-covered box full of butterflies. Whitman, his beard full of butterflies, said Lorca, whose mind was full of moonlight.

Diego created a garden, more beautiful than any I'd seen, and created a home into which everyone could come. My Diego. He was never mine: he belonged to himself, and he was too generous, too universal in his love to belong to me or anyone and, in that generosity, the trap was set. A wall of organ cactus grew between us, and the fountains in the courtyard played instead of us.

In the beginning was the word, right? Wrong. In the beginning, *I was.* I sang one pure white note into the black silence. It was I who let there be mindlight—other light more magical than the sun's, in those lovely days when the world was young. Young it continued to be for aeons:

young it could have been forever. In those lovely days, he used to come to all my parties, he drank too much, he fucked, he jumped burning embers, he played, he stayed up all night and I beamed with pleasure, for then he was truly enlightened: delight lit him, he shone in my light. Now he shuts the curtains, walls me out, he will have no tryst with me. He did not leave me for another woman but for every other woman. This was his nature.

All those who are exiled look to me for their primal simile and I am pale with exile's hunger, having no barley, no hops, no hearthside, no ruddy cheeks. I am sick with an exile's thirst for the bucketloads, oceanloads of water tipping around in giant puddles on earth. Coatlicue is the goddess of all exiled women, all those who shine with too much silver, goddess of both birth and death, her skirts rattle with skulls as she walks and those skulls shine with moonlight and knowing.

My exile forced me to be nomadic, limping across the heavens with bare white feet and, since I never wore shoes, after several millennia my feet bled from walking. I leave bloody footprints now across the sky, and I leave bloody footprints on earth, across the world a million bloodstained bedsheets every month, the footprints of my nomadic courses, which is why still today you can see a million women by a million wells at dawn, washing out the bloody footprints of the moon. I am so tired of walking alone. There is a pair of parakeets at the gate, here a family, there a marriage, with a nest of children, and everywhere they lie in twos while I shine with solitude, bright with its utter light.

But if you look carefully when I am crescent you will see a strange glimmer, the faintest trace of light which only the most observant see at the edge of my circle, the low light of my liminal love, only just visible, only at night, my only intimacy described in shadow terms, like the moon in love with man on the dark side only, on the far and other, the only unlonely side, and only for moments, for when the moon turns a half-inch in her sleep she half-wakes and knows she is alone again, holding herself only in her own arms, morning after night in the bruised edge of the sky.

The moon was homeless, and how many there were who wanted the moon unhoused, hurt by the road, gypsy of the sky whose freedom they could relish only with envy and admire only with resentment. Oh, the moon's used to it, she doesn't need a home, she's a natural nomad, they said, because they wanted her for a symbol of a life they were too mortgaged to lead. (Lorca knew the sadness of solitude, that gypsy grief, and we console each other. My Mexico understands exile, and has a proud history of giving a home to political refugees.) I am exiled from the simplest dream, to lie on a beach in the sun with my head in his plump lap, to swim naked with him, to hold his hand in a taverna in the evening and at night to feel his breath softly fanning my cunt to flame as one would blow on the embers to catch fire, and I can no more have this than the moon could crawl down a duckboard off the roof, balance her toe on the rainwater butt, and hop down to give you a quick peck on the cheek. So I must turn my face away and sing my solo to the cosmos.

I painted *The Two Fridas*, one of me in Tehuana dress, woven into the indigenous earth of Mexico, and the other in European clothes. (We both have hearts too open, and our human hearts are on the left, with its rightful political hint.)

Indigenous Frida holds a tiny egg-shaped portrait of Diego, attached to her heart by an artery which is also an umbilical cord. European Frida, meanwhile, is bleeding to death.

For Mexico itself, of course, it is the indigenous lands which are bleeding to death, and *The Two Mexicos* is the masterpiece being repainted now in the figure of

Subcomandante Marcos, fusing the two. One Mexico is traditional and indigenous, speaking the language of land; the other is Western, speaking the urban poetics of the page. The two marry in the Zapatista rebellion of today, and together they write a message in blood from the open veins of Mexico's heart, for humanity and against neoliberalism, calling all grief-surgeons of the world to help stem the flow.

I have to tell you, because it makes me smile, that Subcomandante Marcos had a crush on me when he was just a teenager; he loved my revolutionary nature and my art. I died when he was still very young, but I passed the baton on to him. *Poet, revolutionary, romantic.*

In the genealogy of revolutionaries, I was fathered by Emiliano Zapata, and I was born in Mexico's earlier rebellion. In the register of births, Marcos was born during my lifetime but, in the register of revolutionary significance, Marcos says he was born in 1984 as the Zapatista insurgents moved to begin training in the Lacandon jungle. (We are all Zapata. We are all Marcos.)

I only have one disagreement with Subcomandante Marcos, and even then it stems from an agreement. We both think that the moon has hope, but whereas he thinks that her hope is to escape her tie to earth, to fly away, maybe to Jupiter or Saturn, I think her hope is to be tied closer and closer by a sweet silk thread to humanity, and that her grief is because of the distance between them. Who is right, Marcos or me? Who knows? Well, without wanting to pull rank on this one—especially against the supreme commander of Mexico's rebel army—I do. I am the moon, after all, in one of her incarnations. Marcos once planned to send a message, on a little satellite, to the moon, saying: 'It would do her good to know that someone understands her.' Yes, and you. It would do you good too.

'It happened many years ago. It is a story of a love that was not, that was left unfulfilled. It is a sad story. . .and terrible,' says the *subcomandante*, pipe to his lips, eyes to the mountains now. He speaks for himself, for me, and for countless thousands, but beneath one ski-mask is another, beneath the Zapatistas of today, that earlier revolution, when my story began, my sad story and terrible, my story of a love not yet fulfilled.

Marcos, they say, is the most wanted man in Mexico. I can quite believe it. Women want him hard in bed, eh, Don Durito of the Lacandon? Kids put on ski-masks and want to be him. But a small and horrible bunch of bankers, bureaucrats and soul-murderers want to kill him, not because he is a rebel leader but because he is a poet. To them, I'd say: Be careful. Would you assassinate the moon? All that would happen is you'd shatter her reflection in the lake, scatter it in a thousand pieces. So too, if you murder Marcos, a thousand shiny coins of priceless heroism will put on ski-masks and climb the mountain under a moon of vehement poetry. Like Lorca, the *subcomandante* writes the poetry of the toreador, and he knows how the bulls of Wall Street have gored the *campesinos*.

There are revolutionaries who dream of bullets and revolutionaries who dream of starlit guitars, on nights when the moon is all you have left to call your own. Tuck the moon into your saddlebag, then, with pipe tobacco, balloons and poems whose fuses are already lit, ready to explode like shooting stars on the skies of ten thousand minds. But all of this is in the future, all yet to come. In my present, I can only tell you that the cords of Lorca's harp were cut with scissors, that my heart fell, the chords of my heart falling down through the octaves below the range of human hearing.

Diego divorced me, and I divorced him. I was entirely bewildered but still entirely in love. But in the terrible confusions of love, there was an eclipse of the moon. How did it happen? Astronomers of the heart could explain it like this: I couldn't take the pain. The loneliness of being flung out of his orbit made me demented for solace. I am a stray moon, and I would swing into the orbit of any consoling planet. So the moon was eclipsed by a passing star. I became exiled not only from him but from myself, and that was my one unforgivable sin, which I regret so bitterly now, because it was a fall from my own grace. I was fatally eclipsed, and I swung away from the truth of my own trajectory. My mind was born winged, but that was the one moment when I betrayed the gift of flight. The best of minds stay faithful to their flight, the wise women, the world's shamans whose transformations are flights of empathy, of curiosity, of curing; whose translations are innocent; who dared to be innocent, who dared to fly, who chose their own soaring. I was unfaithful to my own flight.

What does it mean to fly? To dare to dream. To be deeply, highly happy. And to be innocent above all. I am guilty. I lied to him, pretending I wasn't having affairs. But I lied also to myself, and I misaligned my soul. It is so easy to be guilty, like a goat tethered by an old piece of washing line to a cacky post. It is harder to be innocent. But courage is innocent and now is innocent and desire is innocent and flight is an innocent angle of yearning, aspiring to express the life force, and now I see his eyes shining with flight. Icarus soared, flying in the face of god and gravity. What matters is not that he was forced to fall but that he dared to fly.

Passion above all is innocent. Passion is the very wingedness of innocence, the finest advocate and the only one necessary. In feral tenderness, loving him, cock and cunt, the moon will not be patrolled and she shines free and fearless and there is no sin in anything that shines that fucking much.

I became only more beautiful for being so bruised. I would be a conquistador of pain. I painted myself masturbating and I dared the press to say so. One did. I was all the opulence of Byzantium, and all the spider monkeys of the rainforests. I was saucier than any tart. Like a nutcracker, I cracked jokes till the guests spluttered with laughter like the chestnuts I forgot in the fireplace, exploding like little bombs all over the room. Like, like, like, everything was like everything else. Except him.

I put my special diamond and gold caps on my incisors so I glinted wickedly in three places. Eyes. Teeth. Cunt. It's a display, that's all. The reality is that I hold my own hand, I cry, I drink, I sleep. Skeletons in sunglasses, skeletons in goggles tell dirty jokes around my broken bed until vines and tendrils spring up from my pillows, surrounding me in jungle, my death giving them *fuerza de la natura*. The force of nature: from death comes life. Everything is connected in life, everything spins me into it. There are caterpillars caught in a web which a spider has spun between a green leaf and my black hair. ('Black? Nothing is black, really *nothing*,' I wrote.)

We had a party one day and dressed the cardboard skeletons, some in my clothes, some in his, and hung them from the rafters so there was an alternative fiesta up there; in the commotion the skeletons jostled and swayed and gossiped of the dead and cast the glad eye with their empty sockets and drank shots of tequila through their jawbones.

Enchanting man, he was endlessly enchantable, it welled up, a spring which never ran dry. He was enchanted by dawn and by dusk, every leaf enchanted him, every moment, every river, every tune, every pipe, every wave, every moonrise, every woman. The earth gods enchanted him—as did Jesus, that lovely magician, who shared so many motifs with all the other earth gods, the death and resurrections, the turning worlds of life, death and life again. All of these deserved his enchantment, and were enchanted by him in turn because he was so open-hearted, so free with himself, that flowers crowded flirting into his fingers, rivers nuzzled their courses nearer to him, and for him the stars tripped over the Andes and fell shooting from the sky in the instantaneity of stellar love. He gave himself to the world and the world flooded in to him in turn.

White feathers fall across my window as another sky surrenders.

Do I mind?

Why should I? Like van Gogh, I stand in my own light.

And besides, everything that was ever created loves me. Moth, jaguar, sap. They rise to greet me and I suppose I need none of him, but I am saddened when I see the rainforests choked and rainless. The whales which used to sing for me are scarcer and more silent now. The ice seeps away—the ice which was my favourite landscape—for I was an artist of light before he was born, and I gave ice the brightness of sheer serenity. My sadness now is a cloud around me which I shine within, and no light of mine is seen by anyone else, creating a further exile.

Do I mind?

My soul is broken.

I will have to make shift for myself on the heath of my soul, knowing myself broken to bits and pieces, knowing a howl of utter and lifelong pain. Put out the lights. Put out the moonlight and the suns and stars and then put out mindlight everywhere. This is the Age of Yellow: madness, sickness and fear. How could I have turned from him? How could I? How?

But he did not want me any more. After millennia of tenderly cherishing moonlight, he took the moon out of his pocket and dropped it. So mind, too, slipped out of his fingers and fell on the floor: thought in shards.

And I walked away inconsolable till Walt Whitman whistled to me from the woods. You look like one of mine, he said, and hugged me.

I asked him, are we too few, we of the poet's vintage? Are there simply too many of the others? Those who do not prize either poetry or flight. Who re-cork the bottle before we've finished drinking. Who are a herbicide to the idiosyncratic and a pesticide to difference. Who buy pasteurised verbs and keep them in the fridge, who check their hearts are sterilised, and who, seeing the very liquidity of love, would only handle it with rubber gloves. Who keep the garbage foil-wrapped for freshness but think a vegetable garden is dirty. Who think the volcanic is just another reason for dusting. Who like to titter but never really laugh. Who buy cut-price emotions, a bargain in the marketplace. Who are sociable enough to gather gossip but not kind enough for friends. Who keep their cash safe but freely betray a confidence. Who use their shallowness to scorn profundity. Whose incuriosity closes minds and books and conversations. Who never knew bewilderment or what it was to wonder. Whose self-certainty was as cruelly clean as their curtains, and as surely sterile. Who aimed for the average and scored it competently, who know ambition but not aspiration. Who opt for the ordinary and would sue a bird for singing.

Surrealism. They need it in Europe, I suppose. Their Aztecs are so buried that they need drowned clocks instead. My parrots and monkeys ransack the garbage for real, and jaguars roar from my bookshelves, so why should I look for dream puppeteers?

My Changeling Child in
a World Mad with
Grief

I know Diego of old. I know how his infidelities are a result of his generosities and I know it is who he is. I have watched him a long time, I have loved him, reproached him, hated him and adored him and I think, after all these years, I know him, all his nonsenses, his creations, mistakes and wonders, all his wrong turnings, wit, mischiefs and glories.

But what he did next shocked me more deeply than anything yet.

It was the Day of the Dead and I had taken my sister's children out to the graves which were lit with lanterns and candles, and we ate tiny candy skeletons in their miniature sugar coffins. A merry death day it was, and the children were effervescent and giggly and I held them precious to my heart while we strew *zempazúchil* flowers across the graves and they tipped handfuls of petals into my hair and kissed me and called me *mamá* by accident. For one moment, then, my stomach heaved with grief, knowing that no child now would ever call me mother except by mistake. But the moment passed, and they told me saucy jokes, and we flicked sugar skulls into each other's mouths until the night grew late. We left, turning for home, and burst into the house, the kids fizzing with coffins and candlelight and there was Diego, fucking their mother, my sister.

No pain like it.

No time in hospital, having my bones re-broken, hurt like this.

My sister, my fertile sister, my sister of cradles, not coffins.

I cut off all my hair, as an outward sign of what he had done. I was shorn of what little I had. Take my sister, take my hair, take my sex, leave me only my coffin.

I had just about learned to laugh at the physical pain, the fracture of my pelvis and my broken back, the endless rounds of surgery, being caged in a hospital bed, but the moment I had almost managed to cope, he fractured my heart, making of me an Aztec sacrifice. I was still alive, goddammit, he could have waited. My body was broken—it was fucked—and now my psyche was too. I paint in the poetry of blood and my blood feeds the earth to bloom and to blossom with art.

My sweet sister-earth. And yet he abused everything about her, her love for him, her patience, her trust. I know he didn't mean to do it, but I see the effects. She is maddened with grief. Her rhythms are ruptured and her seasons sundered. Her eyes are bright with pain. And I am not only heart-broken but soul-broken. I would have stayed faithful to him till I died but, when he turned away from me, in my grief I also turned away from him and in doing so I lost my self. I lost my singularity, my wholeness, my integrity. I have made the seas grieve, those oceans which knew the miracle of chance before, the lucky coral as a lively chaos, now only know the dead chaos which leaves her bruised and jangling, and I've heard the seas shriek with pain as a terrible magenta covers the oceans already with the heave of a lifelong grief.

The seas no longer sway with me, but instead they bolt and stagger, they run cold currents where warm should be, measuring the rise of their grief in metres, overflowing with strange tears, as sea levels rise, flooding miles of coast and submerging whole islands. Hurt, the world's waters rage, impotent for the most part but hurling an occasional tsunami of reproach. My gentle ocean is inconsolable and infinite in grief. The coral is bleached, the dugong is butchered and the songlines of the whale are so skewed that one, injured, distressed and disoriented, swam not singingly in the bell depths of the Atlantic but turned right at Casablanca and creaked its confused way to die by the Rock of Gibraltar.

I am in constant cloud now, all passion spent, and I withdraw to lifelessness, grey and empty in a silent shroud.

I paint myself in a double portrait, one of me cut open on a hospital trolley under a searing sun. The other is proud under the full moon. 'Tree of hope, keep firm,' is the banner I hold in my hand. What trees now? Sweetheart, it was in the Amazon that we met, centuries before we were even lovers, there that your gaze swam with intelligence, and I laughed at all your jokes and said, *por favor cuidar este jaguar*. Please look after this jaguar. Meet me then in that *now* again, and again watch the carousel of the sky and, from that turning world pick me, choose me: 'I'll have that one,' and hold me to that warm plump chest.

Life allows so few loves like this. Once, maybe, and if you're very lucky twice in a life, often none at all.

But the Amazon will die of thirst, she will seize up with a drought. An arrow, a feather, an abandoned village of thatched huts, a wizened, drunk old man, crying in a language no one else can speak, crumpled with insatiable memory. One island nation, five atolls and four islands, pacific and named by doves, Tuvalu, is silently submerged as the quiet waters lap its shores, past the fishing boats, up its beaches, up, to the houses at the coastline, on, on, the gentle sea, the sea murmuring in quiet amazement at itself, on, until the centre where it can see itself coming, reflecting its rise, it meets itself in a full circle of embrace and Tuvalu will only be a story of mythic islands beneath the waves.

The opposite death, too, I can see from here, as deserts cauterise my beloved Mexico, I see people's lips dry and cracked, twitching as the vultures soar. I am parched already, but now Mexico is too, and from the plains of Mexico I see people fleeing, driven over the Rio Grande, risking the bullets at the razor wire. Choose your death, a slow death of thirst, or fast as a bullet.

There is a myth that all things wasted or lost on earth are treasured on the moon, which is why all the lost boys end up on the moon. The moon is always what might have been, and I do treasure what is lost, so when the Amazon is gone, it's only me who will remember it, when whole countries are submerged under the sea, it's only me who'll still know their names. I will record it all, *re-cordis*, of the 'heart' in Latin; it will pass through my heart again and again and again. I was, before god was or you, and I'll be there afterwards, Scheherazade of the stars, full of stories of shamans and jaguars and polar bears and firecrackers. I'll be the storyteller of all that happened on earth, but my priceless, precious one, my understander, will be long gone.

It isn't often that I want to tell a story from the land of the future because I do not want to overshadow love with despair, but let me describe what will happen to my changeling child. I knew him when he was a nine-year-old Indian boy from Oaxaca, and he was my disciple, coming to watch me paint. In a few years, he will be orphaned, without family or hearth, becoming a smiling exile, surviving by his loveliness alone. He turns up in a village one day, a refugee from drought and flood, and, smiling, asks a villager where he can sleep. The villager is harrowed with anxiety, his face crossed with worry and sleeplessness, hunger and grief, but this smiling lad is hardly more than a boy—and he will help if he can.

'I have a boat,' he says, 'you can sleep in that.'

So in the daytime, the villager fishes from the little boat and at night the boy makes his bed in it, and is rocked to sleep on peaceful waves. He makes a little money begging—enough to eat tortillas, not enough to build himself a roof or a house. One evening towards sunset, at high tide, an unnatural storm blows in. No storm like this was ever recorded in the village. His boat shudders, gulping in the waves. In one violent surge, with a shriek—no warning, no time—the boat is torn from its moorings, and flung loose to the ocean. The storm rages furiously inland, the child sees all the roofs ripped off from the houses, and the walls crumple like paper, but he can hear no scream, no shout, no panic, for his boat is cast further and further out to sea.

Is there another word for sunrise? the child thinks, but there is no one to answer and, as the night falls deep, the black clouds roll back and it is a full-moon night so he tries to smile at me, but this time he cannot. For the only time in his life, he has stopped smiling, and now he knows exile from everything, even land, and in his strange, sad voyage he wonders now if it could have been different. He blames no one, but he wonders. And he cannot smile. His story is unfinished and he asked me to keep his story safe and—as he was a child of all new beginnings—he asked me never to write the ending as he slipped into an unsmiling sleep.

Shakespeare knew this story, though it was one he hadn't yet written. He knew my lovely little Indian boy, and lent him to Titania, and he knew the chaos, writing it into the play in which he gave me a starry role. When Titania and Oberon were separated, sundered as Diego and Frida, a rift was written in the weather. Unnatural winds rise 'as in revenge' and the rivers 'have overborne their continents', while 'the green corn hath rotted' and the field is drowned. He said that I was 'pale in my anger', and, yes, I must admit to some of that, although there is far more sorrow than rage in me. The seasons alter, he said, with frosts on roses, and sweet summer buds open in winter. 'The spring, the summer, the childing autumn, angry winter, change their wonted liveries; and the mazed world, by their increase, now knows not which is which.'

The childing autumn, I bite my lip to eclipse myself. I do not want to talk about that any more. It is too late.

I swim towards you, drowning in sky.

My mother's skull is wreathed in smiles.

A weird light is brightening me now, a lightness at noon; in the midwinter, there is a twilight which frightens me as the horizon glimmers and, if light could ever seem sinister, this light does. My heart is lit like this, lit with drugs and alcohol, and I hallucinate with images from the future as well as the past.

With my friend the fawn, we pretend to be reindeer

migrating, we run on ice which should have been firm, but now suddenly the ice is cracking, splintering and giving way. Falling, my legs are broken in the shards and plates of broken ice and the fawn snorts with fear, its trusting eyes chaotic with panic. Rolling fissures of ice crack and break with appalling frequency, bombs of ice explode, a soundtrack of war. I cannot tell if this is inside my head or outside.

In the cinema, I watch a newsreel about the Spanish Civil War and they play it with Wagner as the backing music. 'The Ride of the Valkyries' swoops through my head, winged and terrible. The Valkyries, the warrior maidens, gallop together, meeting on a mountain, each with a dead hero in her saddlebag, Valhalla's army, and I think of Parsifal who does not know his own name and his son Lohengrin who is forbidden to reveal his. I have not always known my own name, and Subcomandante Marcos, my son by another name, forbids himself to reveal his.

I came out of the cinema humming this music, even while I was frightened. The Twilight of the Gods was happening in Spain, it was as mythic as that, and I could see a red bandana, a red ribbon running with blood, rippling with pride from Mexico's past revolution to the pride of Mexico today (one of only two countries in the world to recognise and support the Republicans) and to the pride of Mexico's future, where Marcos is holding the faded and torn bandana, with a handful of dry earth. The anarchist-intellectuals flee, eventually, running for their lives from Franco, and where do the luckiest find exile? With me in Mexico, by the light of the sunniest moon.

Stalin drove the communists to murder the anarchists, and began the killings of millions while Trotsky, in exile, came to stay with us. I fucked him. He too had seemed like a kind of destiny, for I was born to the Mexican revolution and as the moon I was born of cosmic revolution and the chief revolutionary of our age couldn't help but feel the pull of me.

Then Diego gave Trotsky a skull of purple sugar with 'Stalin' written in icing sugar on its forehead, a morbid cartoon. Bless him, he didn't see the funny side at all. Me and Diego, though, we pissed ourselves laughing, but not for long, because soon after Trotsky left our house he was assassinated—one of Stalin's agents put an ice-axe through his skull.

I was dying to go to Spain myself, to be part of that theatre of the soul. It was our last chance to halt fascism, but deep within me I knew Capa had glimpsed the future. The first picture of the moment of death was taken in the

Spanish Civil War, and Capa photographed a Republican soldier, shot by the fascists, his arms flung wide open as you would hug a beloved child after a long absence. This was the moment of death for us all.

The Republicans were always short of water, and it was a sere symbol to me, for all the well-waters of freedom were running empty, and the totalitarians, Franco, Mussolini, Hitler, Stalin and Mao, were setting the century on fire, in an inexorable burning world of holocausts. I see the beginning now and dimly I can see the end. It is written. It is written. An apocalypse even of the silky Amazon. A holocaust of all that is moist and green and gladed. *No pasarán!* They shall not pass. It shall not come to pass. If wit and beauty, if grace and poetry, if *La Vida* has anything to do with it. It is written, maybe, but may it not come to pass.

The gentle honeybees in the courtyard have a mysterious illness and are sickening and dying. The Age of Loneliness starts this way, the extinctions of one kind of life after another. The earth is really showing her age, her lands and seasons are out of kilter and her oceans stoned with tempest. The future is galloping towards us, the Four Horsemen, and the apocalypse has escaped like some terrible virus from the back of the book, and is infecting us all. This is a strangely mythic age. Scientists speak of a law of the conservation of energy, but I think there is a law of the conservation of meaning. For four hundred years, myth and metaphor and the meaningful world have been discounted, and only the material was considered to matter, but, believe me, myth will force its way back in, because the mind needs myths, good ones, and it is a matter of mind and mindedness.

Perhaps it began in a kind of leaping innocence; I can believe that—it was a passion for flight above all, the Icarus within. More moon! More sun! Nearer to the flame! The feathers of mind rippling in flight. Desire in the wingtips. Reckless Icarus, yes, blinded by his flight, yes, but oh, what suns in his eyes, wanting to look down and gasp at the lovely turning world, wanting to seize the heavens in courage and defiance, his flight so beautiful and so eloquent. Mankind was made magnificent enough to wrestle with angels, alone, in a long night of the soul, to wrestle with angels and win.

Me, though, I am sick and lame. It is the beginning of the end, I know. Children come to visit me, and I love their visits. Often their parents would say: 'It's because she has none of her own, poor Frida, so she is a devoted aunt,' and send their children to me with twice the alacrity.

I have become so sensitive with illness that even the whine of a mosquito is the Last Post and a siren call. I am juggled like a helpless ball in the hands of Old Baldy, that malignant conjuror, death. I can almost count the number of songs I have left in me. I think of suicide often, these days, and I take more and more drugs to cope, but they make me hallucinate. They also make me long-sighted, and I rekindle my girlhood sense that I will go to the moon one day.

Diego tries to cheer me up by his fatso-dancing around my bed, pretending to be a bear, and I laugh but I am a dying bear limping to the beat of a tambourine I cannot dance to. ('And all the time, we long to move the stars to pity.')

Night is falling in my life.

But from somewhere deep within is a voice which whispers: I refuse. Then it shouts louder: I refuse, I *refuse*. I will find my own *Risorgimento*. The bear which cannot dance must fly, which was why I had painted myself in a robe of wings and given it to Trotsky, my dark lover.

At a restaurant one night, when a pissed idiot accused Diego of being a Trotskyite, he decked the man. His pal pulled a gun and I jumped in front of Diego, in protection, in mother-love, *kill me first*. I tied flowers and ribbons around a Molotov cocktail and threw it to the people on my last public appearance, when I dragged myself to the demonstration against the CIA, who had overthrown Guatemala's rightful government. But these were difficult attempts to make my body walk on the ground, and to keep my mind grounded in realities when it was sick and swimming in flights.

It seems almost a human universal, to wish at some point in your life that you could fly, to want to be a bird. Why couldn't we be content with the metaphor of flight? Why did we have to make it literal? Is this the downfall of the will to soar? Is it written into the story, like the meltable wax? Surely the flight of mind and the shapeshifting of the soul was the real juice of it, flight's true reality was never in its being made material. What is real need not be material at all. In fact, they are often opposites. Why do I need feet when I have wings to fly? I asked, after my leg was amputated. 'For me,' I said, 'wings are more than enough. Let them cut my leg off and I'll fly.' I try to fly by suicide but my wings are broken. I will have to wait for Old Baldy to visit.

I am at the break-point of the soul. For the upward swing of my life, the sheerness of flight, its upward curve into the sky, is about to crash. Flight began in beauty, the flight of the shaman, flying for the moon, the flight of Icarus, the flight of the lunatic who fell in love, who flew in love with the moon, the flight of art and angels.

All that is best in flight is over.

And now, truly, the fall.

I paint myself, I explained, because I am so often alone. How can one woman weep so much and grieve so much? It's easy if you're the moon. And they called me Frida, meaning Peace and Joy, when I knew so little of either, which is a bitter, if unintended, taunt. Someone commissioned me to paint my face inside a sunflower. If there was such a thing as a moonflower, it might have worked, but I painted it anyway, then took a knife and carved at it, scratching, annihilating my own work, my own self.

My hands have become so weak and shaky that when I put on my make-up I splatter it all over my face, and then I see in the mirror what I've done, and my grotesque reflection haunts me. *La Huesera*, the bone woman, is always with me these days, so I paint my own bones and here, in words too, I am painting my broken bones, my broken life, my broken narrative, the bones of my history, written for my indigenous ancestors as their stories lie in shattered bones. And my unfleshed love lasts and lasts like bones. It is over, how can it be? He is gone, but the bones are still with me. I don't know if *La Huesera* can breathe life into them.

They cut my leg off and gave me a wooden leg. I danced the *jarabe tapatío*. I was half-skeleton already and always *Mexicanista*; this was better than skeletons of candy dressed up like me.

I long for him still, and for the vitality I once knew. I ask them to move my bed nearer the garden, nearer the light, nearer the birds whose flight I envy. I am surrounded now by all my paintings, all my creations, at the opening of my first solo exhibition but I am falling and I know it. I have fallen ill, and I think this time it will be fatal. My night of sweetest triumph comes towards the end of my life, my solo show, sung to the cosmos, and the cosmos came to me, applauding, crowding round my bed, the stars loved me, the sun wept with pride. I am so stricken that I had to send my bed ahead of me, and I came by ambulance later, and was carried to my bed, where I lie, dressed in my exotic perfection, drinking and singing all evening long. I am broken, the crescent moon cracked, shattered, clouded with painkilling drugs but I drink and sing along with everyone, from my four-poster bed, calling on a friend to sing *La Llorona*, the Weeping

Woman. Whatever you do, do it gallantly. It's a strange place from which to see the world, a strange perspective, as far as the moon, and as lonely, but in my fallenness I can tell you that, everywhere I look, I see those who fall.

The fallen. The young widow, despairing and penniless in her high-rise flat, gives a party on the last night of her life, she thanks her friends, finishes the vodka and jumps to her death. I painted her flight, to give her soul wings.

The fallen. The psychiatric case. In bed seventeen hours a day, his mind too dulled by tranquillisers to fly a kite or crack a joke. Tamped to nothing with tranx, sleeping the dulled sleep of the torpid: eating jelly and pills. Is this, too, a self-portrait? Under my flowers and jewels, am I the soul limping to its pedestrian Gethsemane?

The fallen. I see these minds which no longer fly. The fallen. Bleak eyes in beakers at parties, in a disheartened tarting for a one-night sop to their loneliness.

The fallen. A fascist priest, rifle to his shoulder in his own church tower, aiming at a nineteen-year-old anarchist. Christ Almighty, is this what Jesus died for?

The fallen. The children constantly chided, the girls with their will overruled, boys with their spirits broken, aged eleven, putting on a suit and tie to go to the office of maths and double chemistry. They fall for it, fall in for life. In step. Hup two three four. The fallen who fell before they ever had a chance to rise. (Though some mornings, shaken awake for school, and still misty with sleep, they look strangely up and murmur: '*Mamá*, why do I dream of flying?')

The fallen. The old man looking blankly back on the nothing-really of his life, the job done a bit badly, the money he chased which sparkled his mind is now got and hoarded, gathering dust in the attic. Sometimes all I can do is curse *El Destino*.

The fallen. In the garden of the house next door, the beautiful beekeeper, her soul the colour of honey, her body humming with pregnancy, lives in the shed and her baby, coming too quickly, is born on the wayside. She alone of all of these looks up at the moon and laughs silver and glad, and she alone is unfallen, she is flying still.

The people of Chiapas are falling into despair, victims of malnutrition and government-issue TB, crying for land and freedom, pulverised by poverty. 'Money talks.' *But only the poor know what it says.*

The Chase Manhattan bank issues a report calling for the Mexican government to 'eliminate the Zapatistas'. The armies of the state flood the Lacandon jungle to capture the leadership, particularly Marcos, that most wanted man in Mexico. The soldiers didn't notice that the moon (the insurgent moon, rebel of the night, first exile of the cosmos) had climbed the ceiba tree, slung her hammock between two branches and scooped him up, holding him tight, saying, 'you're one of mine'—and all that the soldiers found of him was his pipe, still smoking and warm.

Risorgimento

*S*till smoking and warm, the story is not ended, but the end is near. 'I hope the exit is joyful,' I said, for a messenger drawing a black angel flying up into the sky, 'and I hope never to come back.' But this death in this life is a death from which only more life can come. A different life, better, stronger and kinder, and I painted the *Love Embrace of the Universe*. I mother death into life, and life into death, my jingling skeleton got the giggles and fell off the bar stool, weeping hot and real tears.

I can hear the ringing of the copper bowl in the hands of Txati, goddess of breast and grave, whose bowl contains the souls of the newly dead and from whose bowl life is fed. I can hear the bells, the golden bells, of Coyolxauhqui, goddess of the moon.

When I died, they said he looked like a soul cut in two. He said of that day: 'Too late now, I realised that the most wonderful part of my life had been my love for Frida.' As my cortège passed, my mourners sang: '*La Barca de Oro*', the ship of gold. (In the accident, all those years ago, I was like an icon, shining with gold, and now again I am drenched in it.) 'This is goodbye. . .you'll never see me again, nor hear my songs, but the seas will overflow with my tears.' Half-right and half-wrong. He did see me again. As I was being cremated, the heat of the furnace made my corpse sit bolt upright and my hair was in flames, a death-halo around my head, my face in the centre of a sunflower— this end which I had tried to scratch out with a knife but which came to me anyway. The seas will overflow with my tears—well, that bit was right, too right.

My ashes maintained the shape of my bones for a few seconds before the softest whispers of air brushed them away. But those few seconds were long enough for him to take a sketchbook from his pocket and draw my silver skeleton. The pity of it. The tears of it. The death of it. But look again, my darling, look again, at the last painting I ever did, where I wrote in the colour of blood my most enduring faith: '*Viva La Vida.*' Long live life, wherever and however she flows. ('But all should know that I have not died,' said Lorca.)

So fly me to the earth, and if he will create a new heaven there with me, I will find the wings for it. I do not know if he will, or if he wants to, my Diego of undying flight, so I make this as a votive painting, a prayer, a vow, a plea, painting to win him back to me. Always more prayers than artworks, my paintings were ex-votos, and if art is said to mirror life, then I want more—I want life to mirror art, so I will choreograph my images, infuse them with luck and seduction, with vulnerability and defiance, so that they might be a spell to ask for his hand. It was a magic charm, to draw a hummingbird around my neck to draw him to me again.

Start small with a seedling, a kitten, a pun, a note or a bucket of small water. Small journeys on small wings for a flight not small, for the soaring again of an old belief, oldly new, ancient and radical. Do not despise the small, the earthy, there is faerie in that, the glimmering knowledge of earth in whorls, the fertile mind of green, and a translucence of love when everything outside is also inside, green and growing.

Fly deeper into things, fly slowly, fly gently within yourself, for this is how flight becomes sublime and ecstatic. The mind's flight is fire, inflaming and glowing, and I wanted to think with a streak of flame so I dared to soar with the fire of flight, where the perfection is in the tension of tangent, the aim, the furthering—the flaming arrow ever in flight, never wanting the target.

When I write to my friends, I send them scarlet feathers which whisper flight, especially in airmail envelopes, for flight, like love, is magnetic, irresistible and charismatic. All those I have loved the most have a quality of flight.

One whose quixotic flight was spurred by romance and honour, righter of wrongs, tilter at windmills, whose questing imagination gigantised the heart.

One whose soaring quality of flight was to believe in a symbol so powerfully that he became one, El Che, another journeyer, motorcycling the length of South America to find the story for his life, who refused to believe in the power of national armies and who could only be killed by trickery.

One whose flight was audacity on horseback, the political toreador, the original Zapata, taking on the bull of landed interests, seizing land for the *campesinos*, and who, like Che, was assassinated by a trick.

And then there's Chico. I never knew how the human face could smile until I saw the smile of Chico Mendes. More facial muscles than anyone, a myriad joy, Chico lived like me in a Casa Azul, and he was assassinated in that Blue House. His flight too was a journey, the expansion of his love: 'At first I thought I was fighting to save rubber trees, then I thought I was fighting to save the Amazon rainforest. Now I realise I am fighting for humanity.'

They all refused to believe that they were the size they were told they should be, and in this is heroism, through that belief we are all heroic, all those who fly.

One whose heart is so deeply winged I have not seen the limit of it yet. One whose flight is with birds in music as he played jazz duets with a lyre-tailed nightjar. One whose gift of flight is an animism of the ordinary—I've seen her take a glass of water and distil it by pure laughter into silver gin. One who causes daughters to flock to her, lost fledglings which she finds and helps to fly.

These are the loveliest aviators I know and their flights are all forms of rebellion, all ways of re-enchanting. For now the shamans are needed, the artists and everyone who lives by love. What is needed now is enchantment both magical and real; an enthralling both ordinary and ecstatic. And they are all there, on the sudden, a passion of poets, all of those through whom Orpheus lives: Yeats, Emily Dickinson, Auden, Rubén Darío, and César Vallejo, who fought with the anarchists in Spain. Neruda and Lorca sing a duet in Spanish for all the Romantics and Dylan Thomas arrives later and drunker than any, and leans against Whitman's shoulder and sniffs his beard for butterflies while Whitman smiles so fondly towards the doorway that Ginsberg knows he has the welcome of the ages, and they held the moon and came in her arms and cried for her farways always farlove. I saw the best minds of my generating, for their minds were generated by moonlight, these nightwalkers on the song.

I would re-enchant myself with mankind, nothing less, I would put my head in your lap and lap your mist-touched lips which would tell me again what I once knew, that there is nothing lovelier than mist drinking sunlight and no time lovelier than the dawn is now, and in that *now* I give you all the words for sunrise, in all the languages on earth, and I will promise to find the god of new beginnings, on whatever sad shore. In our choreograph of love, we danced on a boat all the way from Mexico to New York, coming to the shore, as you are deep inside me, held, still, one moment longer. Love, my sweetheart, and I shout in tears, crying for how much I love you: so precious it is to love like this, so ordinary it should be, and you laugh and stroke my back.

I will lead you into the sweetest skies of silk, if you will let your mind linger again on the kind side and in this way we will begin again at the original benignity, knowing that every moment is that midsummer afternoon when you were immobilised by the depth and profusion of beauty, when you laughed because you loved each willow leaf as much as you loved me, when you knew, with the purest certainty, that love is the most necessary thing on earth, a re-enchantment between you and everything. Love is not romance. Romantic love (the most that maybe I have managed) is the meanest love there is, that exclusive love of just two people. Mankind was made polyamorous, Pan-Amoric, loving many things, sometimes able to love everything. I love the forests and the flowers and I love women, too, increasingly, these days. But always at my core is you.

Can I re-light this votive flame? In the hearth of my own heart I know a re-devotion to my true *lares* and *penates*, the gods of earth and I require my mind to rekindle its exquisiteness, to re-fiesta every evening, to re-see every dawn, and in cursive love for the seasons to see again how the year nuzzles its nose under its own paw, this lion old in winter, young again in spring, turning in its bed of dry grasses. To tie the threads of thrall again, the re-thrallment of mankind to earth, the lovely tapestry of every corner of the world. The mirrored threads of Rajasthan, tying you to desert song; the faded threads of prayer flags tying you to the floating world; the silk of blue in Mongolia, each thread a skein of holy sky; the woollen skeins dyed in cochineal and indigo, the wool of Mexican rugs, the veins, the roots.

'I am large, I contain multitudes.' I am Frida, and I am not Frida. I am Walt Whitman and Dylan Thomas. I am, of course, Lorca. I am the insight of grief and I am the moon, hollowed out by remorse. My prayer is a novena, prayed nine times to Mary, mother of sorrows. My prayer is from the forests of Mexico, from the molten heart of the earth, from *El Duende* which charges art with power, *El Duende*, the mysterious energy, the life force in its demand for the dark, deep blood-sap. It comes from the strings of the blue guitar, Paganini's violin, Orpheus's harp strings, when veins are roots, drawing up ancient knowledge from *El Duende*, the spirit of the earth. It is unmistakeable, *El Duende*, deeper than politics, wiser than philosophy, to let knowing come from the soles of your feet, warm to the thinking earth, to let your mind be a flute for the moon to breathe through and write with blood as ink so you do not, cannot, falsify.

It takes courage even to say 'blood' in these days ruled by the bloodless: the metallic bureaucrats, the cultural assassins who mock the 'others' for having strands of politics woven into their art, those who sneer, their mouths full of nettles, who killed Keats and brayed about it afterwards, who would silence a Lorca without regret. Malice is in fashion and spite pays by the word. It takes *El Duende*, now, to find the courage for the flickering, self-sacrificial urgency of necessary insurgent art. The best artists are not found in the cliques of cold steel but in those who inhabit the warm world, who hear the blood of the moon humming in the seas and who know the dark sounds of the human body, hearing their own blood in their own ears.

And when there is a re-enthrallment, a re-enchantment, when there is grace in all eyes, there, then, scream the difficult birth, there, release true sky even out of iron.

Then, truly, let there be light.

In the brilliance of that light, all else recedes. There are galaxies reversing away from me at the speed of light, no walls anymore, neither you nor me, just the blinding light of blinding mind, you darling, you sweetheart.

With an uncanny instinct—and great sadness—Plato barred poets from his ideal republic, because they could stir the emotions of mankind. They will create revolutions, it is true; there are explosive devices in their metaphors and their diction is an act of guerrilla warfare. So fuselight and a hundred suns shine for the poet-revolutionaries of Spain and South America, all assassinated.

Liberty light to José Martí, driving out the Spanish colonialists, who killed him at the confluence of two rivers, and who would not cremate him for fear that his ashes would choke them.

'My poetry is a wounded deer
Looking for the forest's sanctuary.'

What light for Lorca? Only moonlight and always the moon. Franco had him assassinated, shot at dawn with two anarchist bullfighters. 'But all should know that I have not died.' And, when the sun on the fields is gold as onions, by that light, Miguel Hernández, goatherd, poet, revolutionary, you are remembered. Murdered slowly by the fascists after the Spanish Civil War, killed by mistreatment because you used your poetry as a flag of allegiance to goodness.

Rebel light to Victor Jara, who sang for his land against Pinochet's brutal tyranny, creating the wideness of wild gentleness, his hands on his guitar were the horses of song across the rolling pampas. They tortured him and broke all the bones in his hands, they tore him to pieces before they machine-gunned him to death. 'Oh my god,' Neruda cried, 'that's like killing a nightingale.' (Keats, another kind of nightingale, was killed by another kind of machine gun.)

A week later, Pablo, it was your turn, insurgent light to your barcarole. Not only a nightingale but an eagle, and the feathers fall across the oceans and rivers, each feather a tiny boat, punting its delicate immense significance to the stream where Marcos sits writing by candlelight the poetry of today's rebellion.

Winelight to the sweetest poet whose sad and kind eyes are forlorn for me. I shine for you. Nothing is lost in light so lovely, my lovely, nothing can be. Turquoise light to the painter of moon scenes whose heart was so open you could see right through her. Luminosity to the composer whose mind has perfect pitch for the tones of the soul, whose bells and clarity ring so pure they transpose from the key of music to the key of light. Skylark light to all those who know time only in nature. One swallow, three, the merry wren. Glistening cuntlight to the one lover and keen cocklight to the other and liplight to both come kissingtime.

Kindlight, kindling light to all mothers, all whom I mother. Mother of all kinds of light, how I mother, for my mothering is stronger than my exile, and my solo song to the cosmos is the *Risorgimento* of an ultimate motherhood.

I had no child. So? I never liked the taste of bitterness; I choose champagne every time. I mother mothering, then, and I drink to it with all my heart. Without me, when would blood flow or ovulation cascade? Mother of tides, I am mother of generosity and generations. Mother of no meanness, no subtraction, no belittling or demeaning, for though I understand the fallen, I never was mother to fallen things: I am mother of the resurgence of their spirits, mother of flight.

And, yes, it is true that if I mother nothing else, I mother the most: I quicken imagination in my womb, I rock thought in my arms, I sing reverse lullabies, twilight songs of such tantalising vivacity that consciousness springs awake and vividly alive, and a curious child in any room will always look at me. A shard torn out of the earth, I was gifted perhaps (or fated) for no mothering except the ultimate, mother of mind.

For I am catalyst, yeast and trouble. I am trickster, coyote and change. I am chaos, tempest and turbulence.

I am mother of courage, mother of the heartroots of courage, of *coeur* and *cor*, the courage to follow your heart, mother of maenads and mischief and glitter, mother of the good joke and the glint, mother of poetry and paradox and fucking, mother of arse and eyebright, mother of passion and booze and friendship, mother of songlines and tribe, mother of Mexico and the bones, mother of Tezcatlipoca, the Smoking Mirror, and the night sky, mother of kindness, hope and ambiguity, mother of Odysseus and the spices of Madras, mother of the Mothers of the Plaza de Mayo, mother of *Los Desaparecidos* and the victims of state terror, mother of circling, chortling and hissing, mother of purring, wiggling and cusping, mother of chuckling, howling and spitting, mother of caressing, kicking and sucking, mother of Zapatistas, rebels and freedom, mother of grace and vehement dreams, mother of saxophone and jazz, mother of Orpheus, the Fool and the flute, mother of wildness, the souk and the prayer wheel, mother of luck, the tightrope and the merry-go-round, mother of aquamarine, scarlet and tawny, mother of shadow and light, mother of time's redemption, mother of moment, mother of rhythm and ordinary magic, mother of eternity, mother of now, mother of day in night and dark germination, mother of curiosity—of charisma—of charm, mother of the sanity of madness and unseen meaning, mother of the roots of words and the truth of metaphor, mother of the significant world and the inner verb, mother—in the end as in the beginning—of mind itself.

Where exile is only another choreography of my love, under a jaguar moon.

Dedication

For their willingness to speak when others
wouldn't; for their sense of compassion
beyond their own lifetimes; for their
vision of the Earth as comprehensive
as the Moon's: this book is dedicated
to all climate-change activists.

For their quixotic courage; for their
willingness to honour their land;
for their poetic knowledge
that truth may best be revealed masked: this book
is dedicated to the Zapatistas.

Acknowledgements

I would like to pay tribute to Hayden Herrera's
biography of Frida Kahlo, which gives both depth
and detail to her story.

My deep gratitude to my agent Jessica Woollard
and Little Toller for their belief in this book.

With love and thanks to those who influenced
this book like bright pigments of colour in running
water: David, Vic, Jan, Ann, Thea, Marg, Bill, Gareth,
Giuliana, Buz, Thoby and, significantly, Penny
Rimbaud.